ALOHA MEANS COME BACK

The Story of a World War II Girl

Laura Ann Barnes

ALOHA MEANS COME BACK

The Story of a World War II Girl

BY THOMAS AND DOROTHY HOOBLER

AND CAREY-GREENBERG ASSOCIATES

PICTURES BY CATHIE BLECK

SILVER BURDETT PRESS

**Library of Congress Cataloging-
in-Publication Data**

Hoobler, Thomas.
Aloha means come back : the story of a World War II girl /
by Thomas and Dorothy Hoobler
and Carey-Greenberg Associates ;
pictures by Cathie Bleck.
p.   cm.—(Her Story)
Summary: Laura and her mother join her
Navy father in Hawaii in 1941, where
suspicion against the Japanese American
residents runs high in an atmosphere of
expectation that the United States and
Japan will go to war.
1.   Pearl Harbor (Hawaii), Attack on, 1941
—Juvenile fiction. [1. .Pearl Harbor (Hawaii),
Attack on, 1941—Fiction.   2. World War,
1939–1945—Causes—Fiction.   3. Japanese
Americans—Fiction.   4. Hawaii—History—Fiction.]
I. Hoobler, Dorothy.   II. Bleck, Cathie, ill.
III.   Carey-Greenberg Associates.   IV. Title.
PZ7.H7623A1   1991
[Fic]—dc20   90-20537 CIP AC
ISBN 0-382-24148-7 (lib. bdg) ISBN 0-382-24156-8

CONTENTS

CHAPTER ONE

A Lei of Welcome

LAURA was the first one to see Hawaii. They had been at sea for five days now, and she was bored. She had already read all the books she brought for the trip, and the only other things to do were sunbathing in a deck chair and watching for land.

She had been standing at the rail of the ship for over an hour. She hadn't seen anything, except clouds and seawater, since they left San Francisco. It was scary, in a way, to think that they were out here on the Pacific Ocean all alone.

She strained her eyes. Something was there, rising above the horizon. She called to her mother, who was on a deck chair nearby. "I can see something! It's land!"

A steward passing by with a tray took a look over Laura's shoulder. He nodded. "That'll be Diamond Head," he said.

"That's a pretty name," Laura said. "Are there diamonds there?"

He chuckled. "No. It's just a volcano. I guess they call it that because of its shape."

"A volcano!" Laura said. She ran to her mother. "You didn't tell me there are volcanoes in Hawaii. What happens if it erupts?"

"Oh, I don't think it's active, Laura," Mother said. "This is supposed to be one of the most peaceful spots in the world."

"Well, then why would the navy send Daddy here?"

Mother smiled and brushed Laura's hair back. "The navy's main base in the Pacific is here. You'll see all the ships going in and out of Pearl Harbor."

"But, I mean, why are they needed if this is a peaceful spot?"

Mother sighed and looked out at the sea. "They're here to keep the peace, Laura. To make sure the United States won't get into the war."

Laura didn't quite understand, but she knew

that her mother didn't like talking about the war. Laura's father was a lieutenant in the navy, and she was used to moving from place to place when he got different assignments. Before San Francisco, they had lived in Maryland, and before that, in Brooklyn, New York.

She knew why her mother was worried. Daddy might have to fight if the United States went to war. It was 1941. Germany was fighting England, and Japan was fighting China, but those places were far away. Most people said that President Roosevelt would keep us out of the war. Laura hoped he would.

As the ship drew nearer to shore, Mother and Laura went back to their cabin to get ready. A steward took their suitcases, and Laura packed the rest of her clothes in her navy duffel.

The ship's horn blew. They rushed out to the rail to watch it dock. A big crowd of people was waiting on the pier below. "Can you see Daddy?" Laura asked. But so many of the men in the crowd were wearing uniforms that it was impossible to make him out. "We'll find him," Mother promised.

At last the ship's huge ropes were thrown overboard, and dock workers tied them securely. The gangplank slid down, and Laura and her mother joined the crowd heading ashore.

As they stepped onto the pier, two young women ran up and placed necklaces of flowers over their heads. Surprised, Laura said, "Thank you." The smiling women were part of a group; when they had put necklaces on all the passengers, they gathered together and began to sing.

"The necklaces are called leis," Mother said. "It's a way of welcoming visitors."

Laura noticed that the necklace droppers were all wearing long grass skirts. "Is that what people wear here?" she asked. She wondered what it would feel like.

Mother smiled. "No. It's just an old custom. Part of the welcome."

Suddenly, Laura was swept off her feet. It was Daddy! He kissed her and reached out for Mother. Laura felt herself squeezed between them. She was happy now. Her family was back together.

Daddy drove them to the house that he had rented. It was smaller than the one they had before, but it had a wonderful view of the sea. And from her own room Laura could see Diamond Head far down the coast. She took off her leis and hung them next to the window.

"It's so warm!" she said. "Much better than San Francisco. Is it always like this?"

Daddy nodded. "All year round," he said. "Ready for a swim?"

"Am I ever!"

They got their bathing suits and were soon headed for Waikiki Beach. Laura had seen lots of beaches, but this was the best ever. The water seemed all different colors. It was milky green in the surf, but looked lilac and lavender farther out. Daddy said the colors were caused by the volcanic lava rock just beneath the surface.

The beach ran along a big curve in the shoreline, so that the waves spread out and pounded endlessly onto the sand. Laura was surprised to see people standing on top of the waves. As they came closer, she realized they were riding on long boards. "Surfboarders," Daddy said.

"Can I try?" Laura asked.

"Takes practice," he said with a smile. "It's not as easy as it looks." But he rented a board from a booth, and Laura paddled out with it.

She climbed onto the board when a wave came in, just the way the other swimmers were doing. But it was like trying to stand on an ice cube. The board skidded away from her, and she tumbled headfirst into the water.

When she came to the surface, she looked around for her board. Another girl was pushing it back to her. "You shouldn't try to stand up on your first time," the girl said.

"How'd you know I never did it before?"

The girl put up her hand to hide her smile, but her eyes were laughing. "You're a howlie." At least that's what it sounded like to Laura.

"A what?" Laura asked.

"A haole." The girl spelled it. "H-A-O-L-E. It's a Hawaiian word for foreigner."

Laura was indignant. "I'm not a foreigner. I'm an American, and Hawaii is part of the United States, isn't it?"

"Oh yes, even though it's not a state yet. But haoles are people who aren't from Hawaii."

Laura looked at the girl. "Are you from Hawaii?"

"I was born right here in Honolulu," she said. "That makes me American too."

"But you look Chinese."

This time, it was the other girl's turn to be angry. "Oh, don't ever let my father hear you say that. He and my mother are Japanese. They moved here ten years ago, just before I was born."

Laura had met Chinese people in San Francisco, but no Japanese. "Then you're really Japanese," she said.

The girl shook her head firmly. "American," she said. "*And* Hawaiian."

Laura was confused. "Let's start over," she said. "My name is Laura. What's yours?"

"Michiko. I agree, that's better."

Michiko showed Laura how to start by lying down on the surfboard. "Then you can just paddle along and wait for a wave. It's too hard to get on after the wave starts."

Laura tried it that way. A gentle wave picked up her board, and she clung tightly to the sides as it carried her toward shore. It was thrilling to feel herself soaring on top of the wave as it curled up and over. But when the board reached the beach, it bumped the sand hard and threw her off.

Laura had hit her head when she landed. She sat on the sand, trying not to cry as Michiko swam in. "You've got to roll off before it stops," Michiko said.

"I found that out," Laura said.

"Try it again," said Michiko. "You're getting the hang of it."

They swam out to where the waves started. Michiko nudged Laura and pointed farther out.

"Watch him," she said. An older boy was standing on his board, making it look as easy as walking. "That's one of the best surfers on the beach," Michiko said.

They watched as the boy waited for a wave he liked. Squatting on the board, he got in front of the curl. As the wave turned, it made a little tunnel of water, and the boy ducked inside it, disappearing from view.

The wave sped onward, and Laura realized it was coming toward them. "Where is he?" she asked Michiko, but then Michiko pulled her arm. "Dive!" she cried. "He's going to hit us!"

Laura was a good swimmer, and she instantly headed for the bottom. The water was fairly deep here, and she pumped her legs till she could feel herself touch sand. She held her breath as long as she could and then swam to the surface.

She looked around. The boy was in the water too, swimming toward his board. Michiko came up next to Laura. As the boy captured his board, he turned and yelled at them. "Hey, you dumb haole kids, keep out of the way!"

Laura and Michiko looked at each other. "You OK?" said Michiko. Laura nodded, and then they both began to laugh.

"He thinks we're both haoles," Laura said.

"Well," Michiko said, "I guess we are, to him. He's a real Hawaiian. One of the people who lived here before anybody else came. They invented the surfboard, you know."

The girls swam together for the rest of the afternoon. Finally, Laura's parents called her in. She said good-bye to Michiko. "I hope I'll see you again," said Michiko. "You staying long?"

"I don't know," Laura said. "My Daddy's in the navy."

Michiko stopped walking and glanced up the beach at Laura's parents. "I'd better go then," she said, and walked off in the other direction.

Laura was puzzled. But she was tired out from all the swimming, and on the way home she dozed off in the back seat of the car. She woke up a little when she realized her parents were talking about the girl she had met. "I guess there's a lot of them in the islands," Mother said.

"Quite a few," Daddy said. "Almost a third of the population. It could be a problem if . . ." He didn't finish the sentence, and Laura went back to sleep.

CHAPTER TWO

Rumors and Suspicions

THE NEXT DAY Laura's father was scheduled to be on duty at Pearl Harbor. He had his own quarters there and would stay for the rest of the week. Laura and her mother drove him to the base so that they could use the car while he was gone.

Laura always enjoyed seeing a new city for the first time. Every town was different, of course, but Honolulu was really special. You never seemed far from the ocean. The wide avenue along the shore was lined with tall palm trees. Downtown was the port, where dozens of ships were anchored at the docks. Traffic was slow because swarms of workers were carrying goods through the streets.

Outside the port area they drove past a big grassy park. Daddy said, "Look up there. That's Iolani Palace, where the old Hawaiian kings lived."

"When was that?" asked Laura.

"Not too long ago," he answered. "The last ruler was Queen Liliuokalani, who was overthrown in 1893. She wrote some of the most famous of the Hawaiian songs."

"Like the one the women were singing when we left the ship?" Laura asked.

"Oh yeah. That was called 'Aloha Oe.'"

"What does that mean?"

"Aloha? It's a Hawaiian word that can mean both hello and good-bye."

"That's strange. How do they know one from the other?"

Daddy chuckled. "It depends on whether you're coming or going. On weekends they have concerts at the palace. Maybe we'll find time to go to one."

When they reached the base, a sentry stopped their car at the gate. He looked at Laura's father's ID. "I'm sorry, sir," he said. "This doesn't permit your family to enter."

"That's all right," Daddy said. He lifted his duffel out of the backseat. "I can walk from here."

He kissed Laura and her mother good-bye. "I'll call and let you know when to pick me up," he said. "Don't get into trouble, Laura," he said, patting her on the cheek.

Mother turned the car around, and Laura watched Daddy walk away. As they started back, Laura said, "I was hoping we could look at Daddy's ship. They never stopped us from going on the base at San Francisco or Brooklyn."

"Things are different here," Mother said. "They have to watch out for spies."

Spies! Laura's neck tingled. She looked out the car window. Three sailors were waiting to cross the street. A couple of Hawaiian girls, wearing long colorful dresses, laughed at a shared joke as they passed the sailors. More people were selling fish, pineapples, and other food from stalls on the street. Women with wicker baskets on their arms were looking over the wares.

"I don't see anybody who looks like a spy," Laura said, sounding a little disappointed.

"Well," Mother said, "they wouldn't, would they?"

They returned home and spent the morning making a list of things they needed. Then they went shopping. They walked down the narrow little street. Each home had a little lawn of rough grass and usually a palm tree or two. Several stores stood at the corner, where a bigger street crossed theirs.

Laura and her mother stopped at a store that had bins of fruits and vegetables out front. In the window were different kinds of fish on a bed of crushed ice. "This looks like a nice store," Mother said, and they went inside.

A Japanese woman smiled at them from behind the counter. "May I help you?" she asked. As Mother talked with her, Laura walked around the store. She saw lots of canned goods that were the same as in San Francisco or Brooklyn. But there were many things that were new to her. Fresh vegetables and fruits that she had never seen before. Mysterious cans and boxes with Japanese writing on them. Candies and little toys wrapped in bright tissue paper.

That was part of the fun of moving around so much. You got to see something different in each new place. Of course, Laura thought a little sadly, it also meant that you didn't keep friends for very long.

Just then, she heard someone call her name. She turned and saw Michiko, the girl from Waikiki Beach. She was carrying a basket of coconuts.

"Michiko! What are you doing here?" Laura asked.

Michiko smiled. "This is my family's store," she said. "We live upstairs. Everybody helps out."

"We live just up the street," said Laura.

"That's great," said Michiko. "I hoped we'd be friends, but I thought . . . well, it doesn't matter. Hey, are you doing anything this afternoon? My brother and I are going to Kewalo Basin to meet a boat that's bringing in shrimp. Want to go along?"

"I'll ask my mother."

Mother seemed uncertain. Michiko's mother smiled and nodded to reassure her. "Very safe," she said. "Nice that our girls are friends."

Mother finally agreed, and the girls crowded into the front seat of an old truck that was parked outside. Michiko's brother, whose name was Aoki, got behind the wheel. He looked almost too young to drive, Laura thought.

"I hope the boats brought in a good catch today," Aoki said. "The dumb navy won't let them work in the best waters any more."

"Aoki," said Michiko. "Laura's father is in the navy."

He looked over at Laura. "Oh yeah? Well, I guess it's not her fault."

Laura felt annoyed. "Why won't the navy let the boats in the best waters?" she said.

"Because they're too near Pearl Harbor," Aoki replied. "They think all the Japanese fishermen are spies."

"They wouldn't even let my mother and me on the base this morning," Laura said.

Aoki laughed. "Well, I guess they're afraid of everybody. But they don't have to worry. The Hawaii National Guard will protect the islands. I'm going to join next year, when I'm eighteen."

"I didn't know they let Japanese in the army," Laura said—and then bit her tongue.

"I told you," said Michiko. "We're Americans."

"I know," Laura said. "I'm sorry."

"All haoles think alike," said Aoki, but he smiled at her.

As they reached the bay, the shrimp boats were just arriving. Fortunately, today's catch was good, and Michiko and Laura helped load two barrels of fresh shrimp into the back of the truck. The shrimp were alive and wiggling, and Aoki reached into a barrel and took out a handful. He tossed them into a box and put it in the front of the truck.

When they started back, Michiko picked out one of the shrimp. Quickly, she peeled off its shell, broke off the head, and handed it to her

brother. He popped it into his mouth as Laura watched in horror.

What was worse, Michiko peeled another shrimp and offered it to Laura. "Yuck," Laura said.

Aoki laughed. "She only likes shrimp boiled till it's hard," he said.

"Oh, it's very good this way," Michiko said, urging Laura to take it. "It tastes like the sea."

Laura couldn't make herself try it, but Michiko and Aoki finished the whole box by the time they got back to the store.

As they helped carry the barrels inside, Michiko said to Laura, "You must be hungry. I'll ask my mother to cook some of the shrimp for you."

"No, that's all right," Laura said, but Michiko insisted. When her mother heard what happened, she smiled. "I know what you will like." She went into the back of the store, and in a few minutes, returned with a rolled-up paper cone. Laura looked inside and saw small pieces of shrimp coated with fried batter.

"Tempura," Michiko's mother said.

It certainly smelled good, and Laura bit into one. "Mmm," she said. "This is wonderful. The only thing I've ever tasted that was even close was Maryland crab cakes. Maybe I can get Mother to make some for you."

"I'd like that," said Michiko. "But I have to work after school during the week."

"Next weekend then," Laura said.

"It's a deal," said Michiko.

But when Laura went home and asked Mother if she would fix crab cakes for Michiko, Mother seemed upset.

"I don't think that would be a good idea, Laura," she said.

"Why not?"

Mother sighed. "I think we should have a little talk, dear."

Oh-oh, thought Laura.

"You see, the reason the navy has such a large base here is to keep the Japanese from attacking the United States."

"But we're not at war with Japan," Laura said.

"We soon might be though. And it wouldn't look right for us to ask Japanese to our home. It might embarrass your father."

"But Michiko isn't Japanese. She's American."

"Well, not really. If Japan and the United States were at war, the Japanese here would naturally favor their home country."

Laura started to object again, but Mother wouldn't listen. "It's all right if you are friends with her, on the beach, but she cannot come to our house. And that's final."

All that night Laura lay awake wondering how she would tell Michiko. She kept thinking it wasn't fair! She remembered what Aoki thought about the navy. Now she knew why.

In the morning Mother said she had forgotten to buy milk yesterday. She asked Laura to go down to the corner and get some. "And you ought to explain to the little girl that we can't have her here for lunch."

Explain! Laura couldn't even face Michiko. She was too embarrassed to go into the store, and walked a whole block farther to buy the milk somewhere else. But when she came back, Michiko was in front of the store, setting out pineapples. Laura tried to hide the bottle of milk, but Michiko saw it.

"Oh, we have milk for sale," said Michiko.

Laura nodded. "I know. Listen, Michiko, I have to tell you, my mother says we're going some-place this weekend. You can't come . . . I mean, we'll have lunch some other time."

Michiko looked at her, and Laura knew that she didn't believe the lie. "I understand," Michiko said quietly.

Laura walked on up the street. She wished she had never come to Hawaii.

CHAPTER THREE

"This is the Real McCoy"

IN THE DAYS that followed, Laura avoided going to the corner where the store was. Her mother still shopped there, as if nothing had happened, but Laura didn't go with her.

Mother enrolled Laura in the local school, but things were no better there. Like Laura, some of the kids were from what people called "the mainland." They were mostly "navy brats" or "army brats"—their parents were in the armed forces stationed on the island. They formed their own little group and stayed away from the Japanese and Hawaiian kids. The island kids, in turn, looked down on the haoles who didn't really belong in Hawaii.

Laura had always hated school cliques. Every place she had been, she tried to make friends with everybody. But here, both groups really disliked each other.

Michiko was one of the Japanese kids, but she never tried to speak to Laura. Laura didn't make any friends among the "brats" either. She didn't like the way they acted toward the island kids, trying to guess which ones were enemy spies.

To make matters worse, Daddy was away a lot. But he finally got a pass for Laura and her mother to come onto the base, and she got to see the big ships. The harbor was filled with navy ships of all kinds—more than she'd ever seen in one place before. Laura spotted seven huge battleships and more smaller ships than she could count.

Daddy pointed them out with pride, and took Laura on board a battleship, the *Arizona*. He showed her the huge guns that could fire artillery shells forty miles through the air. "If the Japanese try anything on our side of the Pacific," he said, "they're going to get a real fight."

For some reason, this only made Laura feel sad. "Don't worry," Daddy said. "Things are quiet right now. I'll be off duty at noon on Sunday, and then I'll take you to one of the concerts at Iolani Palace."

That cheered her up a little bit, and when she got home, she circled Sunday's date on the kitchen calendar: December 7, 1941.

It certainly didn't seem like December. The weather was as warm as a summer's day in Virginia. When Laura went to bed on Saturday night, she left all the windows open. She had a hard time getting to sleep because she was looking forward to tomorrow.

The sound of an airplane woke her up. She looked at the clock; It was not quite eight A.M. Airplanes flying over weren't unusual, but this one had sounded like it was flying very low. She lay back on the pillow, not ready to get up yet.

Another plane few over. The sound of its engine was loud. Suddenly, she heard the sound of an explosion. It was far off, but she could tell it was big. Well, that wasn't strange either. Army and navy planes sometimes practiced bombing on targets towed out to sea. Sunday morning seemed like an odd time for practice though.

More planes roared overhead. Curious, Laura got up and looked out the window. At first she only heard them, but then one flew right across her view of Diamond Head. Laura blinked. It had a big red circle painted on each wing.

She knew what that meant—but it couldn't

be! The plane had the markings of the Japanese air force.

As she stood there, she heard more explosions. They sounded nearer. Laura ran down the hall to her mother's room, but no one was there. Laura found her in the kitchen, sitting at the table.

"Mother—" Laura started to say, but Mother put up her hand. The radio was on, but it was only playing music. "Mother, I saw a Japanese plane!" Laura said.

"I did too," Mother said. "But there's nothing on the radio. There were no air raid sirens. I don't understand." Suddenly, there was another explosion, close now. Laura felt the floor shake slightly under her feet.

"Mother, they're bombing!"

The radio music stopped then. But a long silence followed. Finally an announcer came on and said, "We have just received a report that Japanese planes have been sighted over the island. This has not been confirmed." The announcer stopped.

Far off in the distance, Laura heard a siren. Then another, and another. The sound filled the city. It was like people wailing in pain. Laura shivered.

Then, abruptly, a new voice came from the radio, a man who was practically screaming: "Hawaii is under attack! Hawaii is under attack! This is no drill! This is the real McCoy! All military personnel should report to their stations immediately! Stay tuned. We'll bring you further reports as they arrive."

Mother put her head down on the table. This frightened Laura more than anything that had happened so far. She put her arms around her mother's shoulders. "Mother! We've got to do something," Laura said.

Mother nodded, and slowly forced herself to her feet. Laura saw tears streaming down her face. "You're right," Mother said. "Your father wouldn't want us to be afraid. We're navy people."

"Father's at the base!" Laura said. "That's where the Japanese planes are headed!"

"Yes," said Mother. "He didn't think they would—" Another explosion cut her short. The kitchen window shattered, spraying glass onto the floor.

"That was right outside!" Laura shouted.

Mother looked out the broken window. "That house is on fire," she said. "People will need help. I'll get the first-aid kit."

By the time they got outside, a crowd had gathered in the street. No one seemed to know what to do. Sirens were still blaring everywhere.

Some people had already gone inside the burning house and were helping the family get outside. It was a woman with two small children who were crying. Mother went over. "Is anyone hurt?" she said. "I have first-aid training."

"We're just shaken up," the woman said. "But our house is on fire!"

"I tried to call the fire department," a man said. "But the lines are busy."

"There's a fire box at the corner," Laura said. "I'll go up and pull it."

As she ran up the street, she heard another siren above all the rest. It was a big fire engine, but it rushed past the corner without stopping. She reached the fire box and pulled the lever. A bell inside started to ring, but from the corner she could see the smoke of fires all over the city. The fire department was probably too busy already.

"Laura!" a voice called. She turned and saw Michiko in front of the store. "Is that your house on fire?"

"No, we're OK, but a fire truck just went past. And the fire could spread," Laura said.

"We've got a hose," Michiko said. "Wait a minute." When she reappeared, her brother Aoki was with her, carrying a long coiled hose.

"The radio says all civilians should stay inside," Michiko said as they ran up the street.

"I don't think it's any more dangerous outside," Laura said.

"It is for us," said Aoki. Before Laura could ask why, a neighbor saw them coming with the hose. "That's what we need," he said. "I'll get ours too."

Several other people brought out their hoses and attached them to a spigot in the garden next door to the burning house. Pretty soon they were spraying water onto the fire. Everybody cheered.

Then two more Japanese planes roared over. They were so close to the ground that Laura could see the pilots.

A man shouted, "It's the Japs! They're invading the island!"

Someone else ran out of a house with a rifle. He fired it into the air at the planes, but it had no effect. "They're going to land on the beaches!" someone else yelled. "We've got to stop the Japs!"

Laura heard Aoki say in a low voice to

Michiko: "We'd better get back to the store."

Something whistled over their heads. Everyone in the street ducked or dropped to the ground. With a deafening explosion, it smashed into the front of a house. Laura looked up. It was her house! Thank goodness she and Mother had gone outside!

A woman began to scream. Someone said, "That's where the woman with the first-aid kit took the two kids and their mother."

Laura was stunned. Then she ran, calling her mother's name.

The front of the house was a wreck. The top floor had collapsed, leaving a pile of bricks and mortar. Aoki caught up with Laura and held her. "Be careful," he said. "The rest of it may fall down."

"My mother's in there!" Laura shouted.

"If she is, we'll get her out," Aoki said.

Aoki started to pull away the wreckage, and other people rushed to join him. Laura pushed to the front, and no one could stop her from clawing at the bricks.

"I can hear something," a man said. It was true. Somewhere underneath, the children were crying. "They're alive."

Laura could never remember how long it

took. Michiko told her later it was an hour before they uncovered what was left of the kitchen. The two children and their mother were underneath the big oak table, which had saved them.

But Laura's mother, who had pushed them onto the floor when she heard the shell coming, was badly hurt. Someone tried to keep Laura away, but she knelt down and brushed the rubble off her mother's face.

"She's alive," a man said. "But we have to get her to a hospital."

"Impossible to get an ambulance," someone else said. "The radio says they're all at Pearl Harbor. They got hit hard out there."

"We have a pickup truck," said Aoki.

"All right. Go get it, and the rest of us will make a litter to move her."

"Hurry, please hurry," Laura pleaded. Michiko put her arm around her. "She's going to be all right," Michiko said.

Chapter Four

"A Date That Will Live in Infamy"

THE NEIGHBORS helped lift Laura's mother into the back of Aoki's pickup truck. Laura climbed up with her, and Michiko followed. Someone gave them a blanket to place over her.

Aoki had to drive slowly, for everywhere in the city people had gathered in the streets to look at the damage. Fire trucks completely blocked one street, and Aoki had to turn around. A man wearing a white fire-marshal's helmet waved them to a stop.

The marshal looked through the window of the truck. "Where are you Japs going?" he asked in a rough voice. "Civilians are supposed to stay inside."

Laura stood up so that the marshal could see her. "We're trying to get my mother to the hospital! She's been hurt."

The marshal looked into the back of the truck. "The hospital's the other way," he said.

Aoki explained why they had to turn around. The marshal still looked suspicious, but he waved them on.

"There are all kinds of civilians in the streets!" Laura said angrily. "Why would he stop just us?"

"Don't you know?" said Michiko. "When the bombing started, my father said that people would blame all the Japanese-Americans. He told us not to go outside."

"But you did anyway. Why?"

Michiko shrugged. "Those people needed help. They were our neighbors too."

Laura burst into tears. "Oh, Michiko, and I treated you so terribly."

Michiko patted her hand. "It wasn't your fault. I knew that first day on the beach, when you said your father was in the navy, that we should not be friends."

Laura brushed away her tears. "You're the best friend I ever had."

Finally they reached the hospital, and Laura's heart sank again as she saw the flashing lights of dozens of ambulances. Aoki stopped the truck. He got out and said to the girls, "We can't get any closer. We'll have to carry her the rest of the way."

Carefully, they lifted Laura's mother down from the truck and began to weave their way through the lines of ambulances. Nurses and orderlies were carrying other stretchers with men in navy uniforms. Laura heard parts of what they were saying: "Pearl Harbor . . . surprise attack . . . nobody knows how many men killed . . . ships were sunk . . . the *Arizona* went down."

Laura nearly dropped the stretcher as she realized that her father was in the worst part of the attack. She didn't know if he was alive, or . . . She shut the thought out of her mind. All she could do now was help her mother. "We're navy people," she kept repeating to make herself go on.

Inside the hospital, things were even worse. Doctors and nurses were trying to take care of the hundreds of wounded sailors who were lying everywhere. Groans and cries filled the hallways. And more stretchers were coming in every minute.

After a long time, a doctor came to examine Laura's mother. He lifted her eyelids and shone a light into her eyes. Then he felt her arms and legs. "Broken leg," he said, making a note on a sheet of paper. "And possible concussion." He handed the paper to Laura. "Write down her name and address. We'll get to her when we have time." He turned his back and went on to another stretcher.

"But aren't you going to help her?" Laura said, following him. The doctor said over his shoulder, "We've got too many cases. She isn't in danger. Go home. You're only in the way. The hospital will notify you later."

Michiko pulled her back. "If you don't fill out the paper, they won't know who she is." Laura began to write, and then stopped. "Our address . . . our home is destroyed."

"Put down our address and phone number," said Michiko. "You can stay with us."

Laura did so, but she refused to leave her mother. Aoki looked uneasy. "They don't want us around here," he said, looking at the rows of wounded sailors. But Michiko spoke quietly to him, and he went off for a few minutes. He returned with two Japanese nurses, who lifted Laura's mother onto a wheeled cart and took the paper that Laura had filled out. "We'll make sure she's OK," one of them said. "You kids go home."

Laura let Michiko lead her out to the truck. But when she saw the ambulances again, she said, "My father! I've got to find out what happened to him."

Michiko pushed Laura into the front seat. Aoki started the engine and drove off. "Kid, if you think we're going to Pearl Harbor, you've got another think coming."

Laura realized he was right. She had done everything she could do. But she felt so alone and afraid! She closed her eyes, thinking again of her mother's words. I'm navy people, she thought. I'm not going to be afraid.

Michiko's family welcomed Laura as if she belonged to them. They all sat down to eat something while Michiko and Aoki took turns telling what had happened. Laura didn't feel like talking—or eating either, until she tasted some of the hot broth and noodles with fish. Michiko's mother kept filling Laura's bowl until she was sure Laura couldn't eat any more.

They kept the radio on, listening to the news bulletins. The navy base at Pearl Harbor had been the main target of the Japanese planes. But the army base up north had also been attacked. The American planes at the airstrip there had been destroyed on the ground. No one knew how many people had been killed or wounded.

Laura tried over and over to telephone the base headquarters, but the phone was always busy. She felt helpless. All she could do was listen to the radio. And it might be days before she could find out anything about her father. She tried calling the hospital too, but its phone was also busy.

At 4:30 in the afternoon, General Short, the highest-ranking army officer on the island, spoke over the radio. He said that he had taken full charge of the island government. Martial law was now in effect. This meant that anyone could be arrested by soldiers for doing anything that seemed dangerous. All civilians now had to stay indoors, except for emergencies. No lights were allowed to remain on after nightfall.

"They think Japan will invade Hawaii," Michiko's father said. He shook his head. "Things will grow worse, I fear."

What could be worse? Laura thought. As night fell, she sat with Michiko's family in the dark. The little orange glow of the radio dial was the only light. But still there was nothing to tell her what had happened to her father. Laura finally went to bed, but all that night she lay awake worrying about her parents.

No one else got much sleep either. When they gathered for breakfast, everyone seemed edgy. They kept the doors of the store locked, and there was little for anyone to do.

Then, around seven A.M. the radio said that President Roosevelt was about to give a speech to Congress. "The next voice you hear will be the President's," the announcer said.

Michiko's father got up from his chair and stood facing the radio. He motioned to the others to do the same. "We should show our respect," he said. Laura didn't feel strange standing for the President, even though she never did it with her own family. Now, it seemed like the right thing to do.

The President's voice was familiar. He often gave "fireside chats" on the radio to explain his policies to the country. But this time he sounded stronger than ever before. "Yesterday," he began, "December 7, 1941—a date that will live in infamy—the United States of America was suddenly and deliberately attacked by naval and air forces of the empire of Japan."

Laura leaned forward and held her breath as the President said, "The attack yesterday on the Hawaiian Islands has caused severe damage to American naval and military forces. Very many American lives have been lost." She put her hands over her face, and felt the arms of Michiko's mother encircle her.

The speech was short. The President ended by asking Congress to declare war. From the applause that followed, there was no doubt that Congress would do so.

After the speech, everyone sat down. "War now," said Michiko's father. "Very bad for everyone." He looked at Laura. "I was born in Japan. You must feel hatred for Japanese for what they have done."

"But it's not your fault," Laura said. "I don't feel hatred for you."

"Others will," he said.

Suddenly there was a loud knock at the door. Everybody jumped. Aoki went to the window and looked out. "Police," he said.

Michiko's father nodded. "Let them in," he said.

The men were not regular police. They wore navy uniforms with SP armbands. Laura recognized the Shore Patrol, navy police. They seemed surprised to find a Japanese family here. Then one of them spotted Laura. "Are you Laura Barnes?" he said.

She nodded. "We have orders to pick you up here," he said.

"But why?" she said.

He shook his head. "Those are our orders."

"Where are you going to take me?"

The SP looked cautiously at Michiko's family. Laura could see the distrust in his eyes. He said, "I'll let you know outside."

Michiko and her mother hugged Laura once more, and she went outside and got into a Shore Patrol jeep. They started off. The streets, which were usually so busy, were practically empty. Uniformed soldiers stood at street corners, and the jeep went right through red lights without stopping.

"We're taking you to the hospital," one of the SPs said.

"My mother is there," Laura said. "Is she all right?"

"We don't know anything about that," he said. "We got our orders from headquarters."

Laura was nervous. The only reason she could guess was too terrible to think about. When they arrived, the SPs took Laura inside to the main desk. Things were still busy, but finally a nurse told them to go to room 466. They went up in the elevator. "We're just supposed to bring you here," one of the burly SPs said.

Laura opened the door. The first thing she saw was her mother lying in a bed. She was awake, though her leg was in a cast and propped up in the air. Laura rushed forward, and Mother held out her arms. "Oh, Mother," Laura said, tucking her face into her mother's shoulder, "I was so worried. I called and called, but I couldn't reach the hospital or the base. I don't know what happened to Daddy."

Mother gently pushed Laura back. "He's right here, dear."

Laura turned around and saw her father's face. He was in his uniform, and though he looked very tired, he was smiling. "We have a lot of stories to share," he said.

CHAPTER FIVE

Aloha Oe

THREE WEEKS later, Laura and her family finally went to Iolani Palace. That week, the concert was not a happy occasion. It was held in memory of the more than two thousand sailors and soldiers who had been killed in the Pearl Harbor attack.

But Laura couldn't help thinking of the many things she had to be grateful for. Her father, of course, had been saved. He had not been on board the *Arizona* when it blew up and sank. He found it hard to talk about some of the things he had seen that day. "Nobody was ready," he said, "but everybody fought back with whatever they could. I saw a ship's mechanic throwing wrenches at the planes."

Some of the ships had fired their big guns into

the air, trying to hit the Japanese bombers. Sadly, many of the shells went flying into the city. It was one of these that had hit Laura's house. But her mother was out of the hospital, and even though she had to use crutches for a while, she would be all right.

Laura had told her parents all about Aoki and Michiko helping take Mother to the hospital. The first thing Mother had done after getting out was go down to the store and thank them.

And Daddy had invited Michiko's whole family to come to the concert with them. Martial law had been lifted, and the store was open again, but Michiko's father was still worried. "I don't think we would be welcome," he said. Laura had already told her father about the way people treated the Japanese after the attack.

Daddy said to Michiko's father, "No one will bother you while I'm around. My family owes you more than we can repay."

They all decided to make a picnic lunch. And so, Laura did get to show Michiko what Maryland crab cakes tasted like. And Mother also admitted that shrimp tempura was one of the best things she had ever tasted.

As the concert began, they spread blankets on

the grass. A Hawaiian band played "The Star-Spangled Banner," and everyone stood. Laura remembered that morning when they listened to the President.

As the song ended and they sat down, Aoki said, "I'm going to get into this war. Only three months till I can sign up for the army."

"Why the army?" Daddy said. Laura smiled, for her father always loved the navy. He looked so handsome in his white navy uniform, and now he had a new medal to wear on it. He had shrugged when she asked him what he had done to get it.

Aoki looked embarrassed. "Well, you know," he said. "They don't let Japanese-Americans into the navy."

"I don't think there's any rule against it," Daddy said. "And we're going to need people who can understand Japanese. I know the head of the Pacific code section. If you want, I'll find you a job with him."

Aoki looked uncertain. "I don't want to be sitting at some desk. I want to fight."

"You can fight in all kinds of ways," Daddy said. "A lot of desk people were killed when the bombs fell the other day."

Aoki looked at Daddy's uniform, and then held out his hand. "I'd be proud," he said.

Laura saw Aoki's mother smile as they shook hands. "Thank you," she said softly.

"My son will not disgrace you—or his family," Aoki's father said.

They listened quietly to the music for a while. Michiko moved closer to Laura and whispered in her ear, "We'll all be navy people now." Laura squeezed her hand.

A group of Hawaiian women began to sing "Aloha Oe." They sang slowly, making the words sound sad this time. "This is the song that means hello or good-bye," Laura said.

"I guess we know what it means today," replied Michiko. Laura nodded. She and her mother were going back to the mainland tomorrow morning. Even though the Japanese had not invaded Hawaii, it was thought too dangerous for the military's families to stay here.

"I made something for you," said Michiko. She took a lei out of the picnic basket and draped it over Laura's shoulders.

"Oh! It's beautiful!" Laura said. "What kind of flowers are these?"

"A kind of orchid that grows in the forests up

north. We got a shipment of them from a Hawaiian farm. I hoped you would like them."

"They're wonderful. I'll take them back with me, and when I look at them, I'll remember you."

"Oh no," said Michiko. "You're supposed to throw your lei overboard when you leave the island."

"But why?"

"It's a custom. You see, it's like asking the island whether it wants you to come back. If you watch the lei, and the waves take it back toward shore, it means you will return someday."

Laura fingered the little purple and pink blossoms. She hated to think of throwing them away. "What if it doesn't go in toward shore?"

"It means you will not see Hawaii again. But we will still be friends, won't we?"

"Always," Laura said. "I promise, I won't ever forget you."

The last notes of "Aloha Oe" floated on the air, and people began to leave. It was getting dark, and people were still supposed to stay indoors at night.

Daddy drove Michiko's family to their store. As they got out, everyone said good-bye. "I'll write you," Laura said. "Someday the war will be over, and then . . ."

"The lei will tell you," Michiko said. She gave Laura a last hug.

On the way to the hotel where they were staying now, Laura asked her father, "Will anything bad happen to Michiko's family?"

"Why would you think that?" he asked.

"Some people do blame the Japanese-Americans for the attack. The newspapers say that the military police have arrested some of them."

"Don't worry, Laura. I'll come by and see if they need any help. Nobody will accuse them of being disloyal—especially with their son in the navy."

Daddy stayed with them that night—the last one they would spend together for quite a while. Laura saw that Mother was worried about him but tried not to show it. Navy people again.

But the next day Mother cried a little at the pier when she kissed Daddy good-bye. "Don't worry," he said. "If they couldn't kill me at Pearl Harbor, they'll never get me. We're going to be ready to defend ourselves now."

The Hawaiian girls were putting leis on everyone again, just as they had when they arrived.

But Laura wouldn't let them give her one. She was wearing the one Michiko had given her.

From the rail of the ship, they picked out Daddy down below them and waved till he saw them. People on board threw streamers over the side of the ship and tried to act happy, but all the families knew they might never see each other again. Laura felt the mood. As the ship pulled away, she watched her father till he was only a dot in the crowd.

She wanted to go into her stateroom and cry where nobody could see her. But she had to keep her promise to Michiko. She didn't know when she was supposed to throw the lei, but as the ship passed by Diamond Head, she decided now was the time.

She looked at the big green volcano and made a silent wish. Then she took the lei from her shoulders and threw it out as far as she could.

She saw it splash into the water. It floated, making a little circle of flowers against the deep blue sea. Go in, go in, Laura urged it. Then a swell of water from the wake of the ship picked it up. The lei rode the crest, hesitated, and then moved toward shore.

"I'll come back," Laura whispered to herself. "I'll come back. Aloha, Hawaii."

MAKING A
LEI

THE ORIGINAL Hawaiians were Polynesian people who rode their huge wooden canoes, with sails, across the Pacific. Over centuries they spread through most of the islands of the South Pacific—at least a thousand years before Columbus crossed the Atlantic.

The Hawaiians developed many kinds of crafts using the natural materials they found on the islands. The lei necklaces were made not only from flowers, but from leaves, vines, feathers, seeds, and berries.

Leis became a traditional present for special occasions, and are still given to visitors when they arrive or leave Hawaii. Some are magnificent works of art, made from as many as a thousand tiny blossoms.

Materials Needed

Needle, Thread, Scissors, Any kind of flower with a strong base.

Steps

1. Cut or pinch off the stems at the bottom of the flowerbuds.

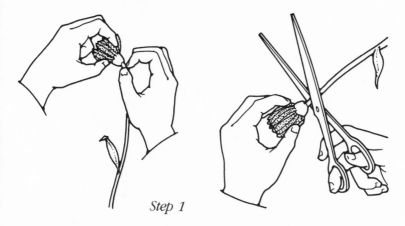

Step 1

2. Cut off a length of thread long enough for the whole necklace. Measure by draping it around your neck so that the circle of thread is as long as you want.

3. Thread the needle and tie a large knot at the end of the thread.

4. Make a hole at the bottom of a flower with the needle and pull the thread through.

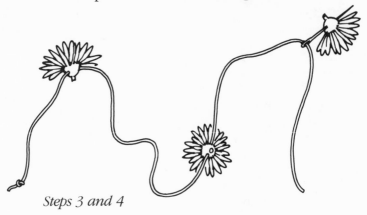

Steps 3 and 4

5. Continue with the rest of the flowers.

6. Tie both ends of the thread together.

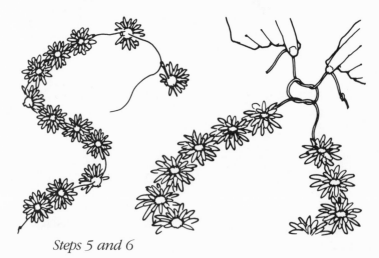

Steps 5 and 6

Tips

Some good flowers to use are marigolds, carnations, chrysanthemums, daisies, black-eyed Susans, asters, coreopsis, cosmos, and zinnias. But experiment with any you can find!

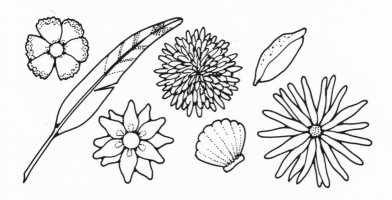

Between the flowers you can add feathers, shells, pieces of wood, or any other material that you can make a hole in. For strong materials like shells and wood you can make a hole with a thin, sharp-pointed nail.